Chapter One

"Aren't you scared?" Jack asked. "I know I would be really, really scared. Horses are huge. They're enormous. Plus, they could bite you."

Lizzie laughed. Her little brother came up with the craziest things sometimes. Second graders were like that. As a fourth grader, Lizzie knew better. "Horses don't bite," she said.

Jack nodded. "They do!" he said. "Sammy's mum said one bit her when she tried to give it a carrot."

"Really?" Lizzie stopped looking out the living room window and stared at her brother. "A horse actually bit her?" Lizzie did not like the sound of that. "But horses don't eat meat. Horses are vegetarians."

"So was the triceratops, but I wouldn't want one biting me," said Jack.

Lizzie nodded. Jack had a point. "Anyway," she said, "I'm not scared."

But she was.

Ever since she had let her best friend, Maria, talk her into taking a riding lesson, Lizzie had been secretly dreading this Saturday morning, and now it was here.

For as long as she could remember, Lizzie had loved animals. Dogs were her favourite, but all animals were wonderful. Penguins, sheep, tigers, pandas – even iguanas! Lizzie loved them all. She loved learning about them, drawing pictures of them, and seeing them at the zoo or on nature shows. Everyone knew that Lizzie Peterson loved animals. What they didn't know is that there was one animal she was secretly afraid of. Horses.

When it came to dogs, she loved caring for them and playing with them and training them. She and Jack were dying for a dog of their own, but so far they had not been able to talk their parents into getting one. At least, not a full-time dog.

But the Petersons were a foster family for puppies who needed new homes. They took care of them until they could find just the right owners for each puppy. They had fostered three puppies so far, and Lizzie and Jack had fallen in love with each one.

Puppies were a lot of work, but they were so much fun! Lizzie could play with a puppy all day and never get upset if it gave her little bites with its needle-sharp baby teeth.

But a horse?

That was a different story.

Jack was right. Horses were huge. A horse couldn't curl up and sleep on your lap, the way a puppy did. You couldn't tell *what* a horse might do. It might kick, or buck, or . . . bite.

Lizzie shuddered. She peeked out the window again, watching for Maria's dad's blue car. It would be pulling into the driveway any minute.

They were picking her up on their way to the stable. Maria was so excited that Lizzie was finally coming with her. She *loved* horses and had been riding since she was three years old. She even had all the right riding clothes: boots, funny trousers called jodhpurs, and a helmet.

"My parents will never agree to buy me all those special clothes just for riding," Lizzie had told Maria. She'd been hoping to get out of going to the stable. But that excuse didn't work.

"That's no problem," Maria had answered. "You can just wear jeans and trainers. Kathy does require all her students to wear helmets, but I have an extra one you can borrow."

Kathy was Maria's riding teacher. She and her husband, Wayne, owned the stable and lived next to it. Lizzie had been hearing about Kathy for weeks: how nice she was, how much she knew about horses, what a great teacher she was. Maria just *knew* that Lizzie would love Kathy – and the stable and the horses – just as much as she did.

4

Lizzie was not so sure. But she had decided that the best way to deal with her fear was to face it, and that meant going to the stable with Maria, meeting Kathy and – *eek!* – climbing on to a horse and riding it.

Every time she thought about that, Lizzie's hands got sweaty and her heart started to pound.

"Everything OK, sweetie?" Lizzie's mum came through the living room, chasing after the Bean, Lizzie's youngest brother. The Bean (his real name was Adam, but nobody ever called him that) liked to pretend he was a dog. At the moment, he had a stuffed toy in his mouth and he was crawling fast. He was playing keep-away from Mum. Mum stopped and gave Lizzie a curious look. "You must be excited about your riding lesson."

"I guess," said Lizzie, shrugging.

"You're a brave girl," her dad said. He had come into the room with the morning newspaper – the one that her mum was a reporter for – and he was sitting down on the couch. "Personally, I've always been a little bit afraid of horses. They're just so *big*."

Jack went over and gave his dad a high five. "That's exactly what I told her," he said.

Lizzie stared at her dad. He was a grown man, a firefighter! She'd never imagined he was afraid of anything, much less horses. If *he* was scared. . . For a second, Lizzie thought about changing her mind. All she had to do was admit to her parents that she was terrified. They wouldn't make her do something that scared her.

Then she heard a car in the driveway. "That must be Maria!" she said. It was too late. Now she had to go through with it. But as she was walking towards the front door, she heard a dog barking. It was a loud, piercing, high-pitched bark. "That's not Simba," she said. Maria's mother was blind, and Simba was her guide dog. He was a big, calm yellow Labrador retriever who hardly ever barked at all.

Lizzie opened the front door and saw a car in

the driveway. But it wasn't a blue one. It was green. There was a woman getting out of the car. In one hand she held a bag of dog food. In the other, she held a red leather leash. And at the end of the leash was an adorable puppy. It was white, with patches of black and tan. It was jumping straight up and down as if all four legs were pogo sticks. *Boing! Boing!* And it was barking its little head off.

By now, Lizzie's family was standing behind her at the open door. They were all staring at the puppy.

"Please!" exclaimed the woman. "You have to help me."

CHapter TWo

"That's Susan, from work," Mrs Peterson said. "Susan?" she asked the woman. "What are you—"

"I can't take it any more," said the woman. "We tried. We really did. But we just can't deal with this dog." She had to shout to be heard over the puppy's barking.

At the same time, a baby in a car seat inside the car started to wail, and the two blond little kids strapped in next to him began to yell, "Mummy, Mummy, Mummy!"

Lizzie walked over to the woman and took the leash from her hand. "Come on, pup," she said, leaning down to scoop the excited puppy into her arms. "Quiet down. *Shh, shh,* you're being silly."

Let me down! Let me down! Let me down! The puppy wriggled and barked. What good was being in a new place if you couldn't explore? Oh, well, if he couldn't get down, maybe he could at least make a new friend!

The puppy struggled a little, but then seemed to decide that he liked being in Lizzie's arms. He gave a few last barks before he started to lick her face instead. Starting at her chin, he worked his way up to the inside of her nostrils, which made Lizzie giggle because it tickled so much. She couldn't believe how friendly the little guy was.

After a grateful smile at Lizzie, the woman had turned back to the car to talk to her children. "It's OK, guys," she said. "These people will take good care of Rascal." She unbuckled the kids' seat belts so they could climb out of the car, and took the baby out of his car seat, settling him on her hip.

"Rascal!" Lizzie loved that name. It was perfect for the wild little puppy.

Mum came over to give the woman a hug. "Susan works with me at the paper," she explained to the rest of the family. "She's a proofreader there. She catches all the mistakes in the articles I write."

By then, Jack had joined Lizzie. He was stroking Rascal's wiry coat. "What kind of dog is Rascal?" he asked.

"He's a Jack Russell terrier," said Lizzie and Susan at the same time.

Lizzie had recognized Rascal's breed the mument she saw him. He looked just like the Jack Russell on her "Dog Breeds of the World" poster: small and muscular, with a short, stubby tail. His ears stood up halfway and then flopped over, and he had a sharp, pointy black nose and bright, shiny black eyes. He was curious and ready for action!

Susan nodded at Lizzie. "So you've heard of this breed. I never had, until my kids saw one in the movies. Once they saw that dog, they bugged me and bugged me and bugged me to get a Jack Russell terrier. They thought it was the cutest dog they ever saw."

"Jack Russells are definitely adorable," Lizzie agreed.

"So we went to a pet shop and picked out this puppy," Susan went on. "He seemed like the friendliest one in his litter."

"A pet shop?" Lizzie knew that pet shops were not the best place to buy puppies. If Susan had got her puppy from a breeder or a shelter, she would have learned a lot more about what to expect from a Jack Russell. Those dogs were all energy!

Susan nodded. "I know, that probably wasn't so smart. But the kids wore me down."

"How old is Rascal?" Jack asked.

11

"About six months old," Susan told him.

By this time, Rascal was ready to get down. He started churning his legs so much that Lizzie finally bent over and put him on the ground. He ran right over to the flower bed and pounced on a red tulip, pulling Lizzie along.

"Hey!" said Mr Peterson. "Lizzie, keep him out of the garden."

Lizzie tugged on the leash, but Rascal ignored her. He pounced on a yellow tulip, and then on another red one. He was so cute and funny to watch that for a mument they all just stood there laughing. But finally Lizzie picked him up and set him down on the lawn, away from the garden.

Hey! What's the big deal? I was having fun! Rascal twirled around three times to the right and three times to the left, then jumped straight up in the air a few times, barking the whole time. By the time he finished, he'd forgotten all about the tulips.

Yahoo! The soft grass felt great under his feet. Life was good.

"Anyway, he's a sweet guy, so friendly and happy. But he's also been nothing but trouble since we got him," Susan was saying. "He barks. He jumps all over the furniture. He chases the neighbour's cat. He chews everything, and he doesn't listen to a thing I say." She jiggled the baby she was holding. "I just can't deal with him any more. I have three kids to take care of, too."

"We'll take him!" Jack said. He was on his knees next to Rascal. Lizzie was holding the puppy's leash, and Jack was trying to get him to shake hands.

"Whoa, wait a minute, kiddo," said Mum. "I'm not so sure about that."

"But you told me all about how you found homes for those other puppies!" said Susan. "I was hoping you could do the same for Rascal."

"Yeah! Please, Mum?" Lizzie said. "We don't have to keep him for ever. We can just be his foster family until we find the right home for him." She looked down at the puppy, who was chewing on Jack's shoelaces. He really was pretty cute for a little dog. Usually Lizzie liked big dogs much better, but Rascal seemed like such a fun puppy – even if he did have a lot of bad habits. "I'm sure we can train him so he'll behave better."

"The kids have done a tremendous job with the other puppies we've fostered," Dad reminded Mum.

"I know," Mum said. "But this puppy really seems like a lot of work."

"He's completely house trained," Susan said. "He *never* makes mistakes."

"See, Mum? He's smart," Lizzie said. "He'll learn fast. He just needs more attention than Susan can give him."

"Well," Mum said slowly. "If you're really ready to take this puppy on. . ."

"Yay!" yelled Lizzie and Jack together. Rascal sprang to his feet and spun around, barking.

Just then, a blue car pulled into the driveway. "Maria!" Lizzie said. She had forgotten all about the riding lesson – and now she had the perfect excuse to put it off. Obviously, she was going to have to stay home and help with the new pup.

Rascal the troublesome puppy had arrived at just the right time.

Chapter Three

Lizzie had recently read that it was a good idea to keep a diary for dog training, so she decided to start one for Rascal.

Training diary: Rascal

Day One, Saturday

Here goes. Rascal arrived today. He sure is full of energy! After about ten minutes indoors, Mum begged us to take him outside. Sammy came over to help me and Jack figure out the best way to help Rascal get rid of his bad habits. . . .

"So, this is the new puppy?" Sammy watched as Rascal tore around the yard, barking at everything and nothing. Sammy, Jack's best friend, lived next door.

"Good thing I didn't bring Rufus and Goldie," said Sammy. "I think you have your hands full already." Rufus was an older golden retriever, and Goldie was a younger one. Goldie was the first puppy the Petersons had ever fostered. It had been really hard to give her up, but at least she now lived right next door.

"I don't know." Lizzie sighed. "Maybe they would be a good influence on Rascal. He's out of control!" Lizzie had learned a lot about training dogs – from the Internet, from books, and from dog trainers she had met – but she wasn't sure any of it would work with this puppy. He definitely had a mind of his own, and enough energy for a whole *pack* of dogs.

"Mum sure wasn't happy when he ran into the living room and jumped on to the couch," Jack agreed.

"And from the couch to the chair to the coffee table," Lizzie added. "I don't think his feet touched the floor once."

*   *   *

Rascal wondered why nobody was chasing him. It was fun to run around in circles, but much more fun when somebody chased you. He barked some more. Why weren't the children playing with him?

Rascal dashed towards Lizzie and away again, looking over his shoulder. "He wants me to chase him," Lizzie said. "But there's no way I'm getting into that game. He needs to learn that the best way to get my attention is to come over and sit quietly."

"Ha!" said Jack. "Like he'll ever do that!"

"If we wait long enough he might," Lizzie said. "And if he does, he'll get a biscuit." She showed Jack and Sammy the dog biscuits in her pocket. "That's called positive reinforcement. If he does something good, he gets a treat. The books say it will work better than yelling at him."

"Hmm," said Jack. "Maybe we should tell Mum about positive reinforcement. If I got ice cream for finishing my homework, I'd probably do it sooner."

"I think my mum already knows about it," said Sammy. "She promised me a new baseball glove if I keep my room clean for a month."

While they were talking, Rascal had finally stopped barking and running around the yard. Lizzie could tell that he was looking at her. She pretended not to notice. He came closer, cocking his head curiously. She kept pretending to ignore him. Finally, he sat right down next to her.

"Good dog!" Lizzie exclaimed. She tossed him a dog biscuit.

Rascal jumped up and snatched it out of the air. He gobbled it down. Then he took off again at high speed.

"Well," Lizzie said, laughing as she shook her head, "it's a start, anyway."

Training Diary: Rascal

Day Two, Sunday

Here is a list of some of the things Rascal has chewed in the 24 hours since he came to stay with us:

The straps on Jack's backpack.

Dad's favourite work gloves.

(Right glove totally destroyed. Left one still sort of wearable, but missing thumb.)

Lizzie's maths book.

(Not that I mind.)

The Bean's yellow blankie.

Mum's new sandals.

There were more items Lizzie could have added to the list, but it was too depressing. Rascal's chewing habit was a real problem. On Sunday morning, after Mum found her sandals – or what *used* to be her sandals – on the bathroom floor, Lizzie got on to the Internet to do some research. What was the best way to train a puppy not to chew?

The first thing Lizzie learned was: don't give the puppy a *chance* to chew things. After lunch, she and Jack and Dad closed off the kitchen with one of the Bean's old baby gates. From now on, Rascal would have to stay in there. If he couldn't roam the house, he would have fewer chances to find things to chew.

"Plus, he won't be able to jump all over the furniture," Jack told Lizzie. Rascal looked back at them from inside the kitchen. He whined and barked and jumped up and down.

Lizzie had also learned that it was a good idea to give a puppy his *own* things to chew on, toys that were made for a little dog with sharp teeth. She tossed Rascal a puppy-sized rawhide bone. He scrambled after it and sat under the kitchen table, gnawing happily.

If only they had given me this yummy bone in the first place, thought Rascal. This was way, way better than any of the other things he'd tried to eat. And nobody was going to take it away from him, either. He was safe and sound in the kitchen, behind the gate. Life was good.

Lizzie shook her head as she watched Rascal chew. She had never imagined that she would meet a dog she couldn't train. But Rascal was a real challenge.

Chapter Four

"Rascal sounds like a handful." Maria offered Lizzie a Fig Newton from her lunch bag.

"He is," Lizzie said. She took the cookie and started nibbling off the edges. Then she sighed. "I hate to admit it, but I'm not even sure what to do with him next." She had already given up on the training diary. It was just too upsetting to have to write down every naughty thing Rascal did. Dealing with Rascal was a full-time job, and after only two days it was wearing her out. Being at school was almost like a holiday.

"Maybe you just need a break," Maria said. "I have a riding lesson after school. I bet Kathy could fit you in if you wanted to come."

Lizzie shook her head and popped the last bite of Fig Newton into her mouth. "I can't," she said, scrunching up her lunch bag. "We signed Rascal up for puppy kindergarten and it starts today."

"Puppy kindergarten?" Maria laughed. "What do they do, finger-paint and play with blocks?"

Lizzie giggled, picturing puppies tracking finger-paint all over. Or would that be paw-paint? What a mess! "No, it's just a series of classes to teach puppies basic obedience, like how to sit and walk on a leash. They also get used to being around other dogs. It'll be fun."

And it did look like fun when Lizzie and Jack arrived at puppy kindergarten later that day. Dad dropped them off at the Littleton recreation centre, promising to come back in time to watch the last ten minutes of class.

Rascal pulled hard at the leash when he heard the sound of barking dogs. He practically dragged

Jack up the stairs. "Hey!" Jack yelled. "Take it easy!"

"Looks like someone needs to learn some leash manners," said a college-age girl who was arriving at the same time. She stuck out her hand. "I'm Jamie, your teacher. And this is. . .?"

"Rascal," Lizzie said. "We signed him up yesterday. We just got him on Saturday."

"Oh, right," said Jamie. "You're the family that's been fostering puppies. Jack and Lizzie Peterson, right? I've heard all about you. Isn't one of your puppies going to be a guide dog?"

Jack and Lizzie exchanged a look. They were getting famous for fostering puppies! Cool. Lizzie nodded. "That was Shadow," she said. "Our last foster pup."

"That's awesome," said Jamie. "Good for you."

She pushed open the door to the gym, and the barking got louder. "Oh, wow," Lizzie said when she saw all the puppies. There were six of them —

no, seven! Eight! They were running and tumbling and wrestling and biting one another. One of them, a tiny brown dachshund, was peeing in the corner while its owner chatted with the owner of a baby bulldog.

"Oops," Lizzie said, pointing to the mess.

Jamie shrugged and pulled a roll of paper towels out of her tote bag. "It's all part of puppy kindergarten," she said.

"You can let Rascal off his leash," Jamie added as she headed over to clean up the puddle. "We keep the door shut so the puppies can play safely when they first arrive. That way they burn off some energy."

"But –" Lizzie began. She wasn't sure how Rascal would get along with other dogs. They had decided to wait a few more days before introducing him to Goldie and Rufus.

"Just keep an eye on him!" Jamie called as she went to talk to another owner.

"OK, Rascal, here you go!" Jack said, removing the leash.

Yahoo! Freedom at last! That leash thing was horrible. Didn't they understand that he needed to run and play? Plus, he had a job to do. He had to let all these other dogs know who was in charge.

The second he was free, Rascal dashed away, zooming around the gym. He ran up to one puppy after another, pouncing on each of them and making it clear that he was the boss. The tiny dachshund pounced right back, but the bigger bulldog trembled in fear, backing up against his owner's legs. Next Rascal jumped on a black Lab puppy, and an Alsation with gigantic ears, and two poodles, one black and one white. Rascal stole a squeaky football toy from a shaggy black pup and chased a funny corgi puppy with short legs under the bleachers.

Lizzie and Jack chased all over the gym after Rascal, trying to keep him from scaring the other puppies. "Rascal!" Lizzie cried. "Be nice!"

"Come on, Rascal," Jack pleaded. "Can't you be friendly?"

Soon Lizzie was completely out of breath.

"OK, everybody, let's leash our pups and get started," Jamie called from the middle of the gym floor.

"Ha," said Jack. "Like *that's* going to be easy." He and Lizzie had already learned that it was tricky to catch Rascal if he didn't want to be caught.

"Come here, you!" Lizzie said. She tried to grab Rascal as he flew past her towards the cowardly bulldog. It was so embarrassing. All the other owners were already standing in a big circle with their puppies. They were ready to work.

Finally, Jamie sneaked up on Rascal while he was trying to wrestle with the shaggy black puppy. She hung on to his collar until Lizzie could snap his leash on. "Thanks," Lizzie said, blushing.

"No problem," Jamie said. "He's just a wild child. That's why he's at puppy kindergarten, right?" She smiled at Lizzie.

But an hour later, she wasn't smiling as much. Rascal barked when Jamie was trying to talk, chased the other puppies during leash-walking practice, and tried three more times to steal the black puppy's squeaky toy. "Rascal," Jamie finally said, "I think you need a time-out." She asked Lizzie and Jack to take him outside for a few minutes and let him "cool down".

Lizzie almost didn't want to go back inside when the time-out was up. But Rascal needed training, and Lizzie needed help! "I'm really sorry," she said to Jamie when class was finally over. "Maybe we shouldn't come back next time." Was Rascal going to be a kindergarten dropout?

"Oh, don't worry about it," Jamie said. "You should definitely keep trying. Believe me, I've seen worse. He'll learn!"

Lizzie was starting to wonder about that.

Chapter Five

"Almost there!" Maria bounced up and down on the seat as her dad's blue car rumbled down a long, bumpy dirt driveway. "I can't believe you finally made it to the stable!"

"Me neither," Lizzie said, hoping that the nervousness in her voice sounded more like excitement. Her first riding lesson was finally about to happen! Her mum had insisted that Lizzie deserved a break from Rascal, so she couldn't use *that* excuse any more. Within a half-hour she was going to be on the back of some gigantic horse. If she was lucky! If she was unlucky, she'd be lying in the dust after being bucked off. Lizzie shivered. Just thinking about it made her heart beat harder.

"You are going to *love* it here, I promise," Maria babbled on. "Everybody's so friendly, and the horses are the best. And Kathy is so, so cool! She knows everything there is to know about riding and caring for horses. Remember how I told you about that one horse, Tony, who hurt his leg? Kathy and Wayne have been taking care of him, and he's almost ready to ride again."

"Great," Lizzie said. Maria barely seemed to notice whether she said anything or not. Her friend was so excited that she just kept talking. Lizzie wasn't even sure which of the names Maria mentioned belonged to horses and which were people. Sally, Frankie, Tony, Kathy, Vanessa, Pokey, Sir Galahad... The names just blended into one another.

"Hey, gal, slow down," Maria's father said, patting his daughter on the shoulder. "Give Lizzie a chance to get to know the place in her own way."

But Maria just kept bouncing in her seat. "Here we are!" she sang out as the car pulled to a stop in front of a weathered old barn. Next to it was a riding ring, a dusty circle of dirt enclosed by a wooden fence. And next to that was the paddock, the grassy area where the horses grazed.

"Look, there's Tony!" She pointed to a white horse with big black spots. He was yanking grass out of the ground in the paddock, whisking his long black tail as he chewed. "He's a paint. You know, like an Indian pony? Tony!" she called. She made a clucking noise with her tongue as she and Lizzie climbed out of the car, and Tony came trotting over.

Maria's dad waved and drove off. Lizzie watched him go, wishing she were still in the car.

Maria handed Lizzie a big carrot. "Here, give him this and he'll love you for ever," she said.

Lizzie stood frozen in place.

"Go ahead," Maria said. "He won't hurt you."

Lizzie laughed nervously. "I know that," she said. "Here, I'll go first." Tony's teeth looked awfully big when he took Maria's carrot.

Tony reached his nose through the fence and bumped it against Lizzie's arm. "Hey!" she said.

"He just wants your carrot," Maria told her.

Carefully, Lizzie held out the carrot the way she had seen Maria do it, on her flat, outstretched hand. Tony took it gently. Lizzie didn't feel a thing except his warm breath on her hand. She could smell his horsey smell now that she was up close to him, and she kind of liked it. His coat was shiny, and his nose looked as soft as velvet.

"You can pat him," Maria urged.

Slowly, Lizzie reached up a hand and patted Tony's neck. His ears twitched and he blew out some air as he leaned towards her. She pulled away. But she wasn't really scared. Maybe some horses were mean, but Tony was obviously harmless and sweet.

"He likes you!" Maria said.

"Has Tony ever met anyone he *didn't* like – especially if they give him carrots?" A woman in jeans and a blue work shirt had come up next to them. She was smiling. "You must be Lizzie," she said, sticking out her hand. "I'm Kathy. Glad to see you here."

"She can ride today, right?" Maria asked.

Kathy paused for a second and looked Lizzie over. "Sure," she said. "I think she'd enjoy riding Sally, don't you?"

"Perfect," agreed Maria. "I'll go tack her up."

Lizzie pictured a big horse tacked to a bulletin board. "What?" she asked.

"I'm going to put on her saddle and bridle," Maria explained. "That stuff is called tack." She pulled Lizzie by the hand. "Come on, I'll show you how to do it. Next time you can get your own horse tacked up."

Lizzie followed Maria into the dark, shady barn. It smelled musty and sweet, like hay and horses and leather. Lizzie took in a deep breath as she walked down the aisle with Maria. Horses leaned over their stall doors to nicker hello, and Maria told Lizzie everyone's name, pointing to the hand-carved signs nailed up by each stall.

"That's Willie, and Jasper, and Treasure," she said. "The black one is Jet. She's a little skittish."

"I like this one," Lizzie said, looking at a golden horse with a pale gold mane.

"That's Minx. She's a palomino. Isn't she gorgeous?"

Sally turned out to be a sweet grey horse, not too big, and very friendly. Maria took Lizzie into the tack room to grab a saddle and bridle, and back into the stable to walk Sally out of her stall. The mare waited patiently while Maria gave Lizzie a lesson in putting on a saddle, showing her how to check if the girth was tight enough. Then Sally let Lizzie walk her out towards the riding ring.

Kathy met them at the barn door. "Up you go," she said, pointing to a large step. "You can stand on that block to make it easier."

Lizzie hesitated.

"Go ahead," said Kathy. "Just put your left foot into the stirrup and throw your right leg over her back. She'll stand there all day until you're ready, but the sooner you get on, the sooner you can be riding."

Before she knew it, Lizzie was sitting high up on Sally, riding her around the ring at an easy, slow walk while Kathy guided the horse with a long rope called a lead line. Kathy said encouraging things like, "Great! Keep your heels down and your head up. Elbows out! Excellent!"

"You look great on her!" Maria said. She was grinning from ear to ear.

So was Lizzie. Riding had definitely taken her mind off Rascal. To her surprise, she was having the best time ever!

Chapter Six

"Rascal, no!" Lizzie could not believe how many times she had said those words in the last ten minutes.

She and Rascal and Jack were at puppy kindergarten again. They were trying their best to follow Jamie's directions.

Well, Lizzie and Jack were trying to follow directions. Rascal? He was just trying to cause as much trouble as possible, or at least that's the way it seemed.

"How could you be so smart and so cute, but also be such a pest?" Lizzie asked the puppy. They were supposed to be practising walking on a leash. All the owners and puppies were going in a big circle around the gym.

Rascal had already barked at the bulldog puppy, chased the dachshund, and pounced on the Lab puppy and both poodles. And not during playtime, either. He had done all that during the lesson on "sitting".

Now they were trying to walk, but he kept grabbing the leash in his teeth and shaking it, growling his little puppy growls.

Grrr, grrr. Rascal was teaching that leash a lesson. Silly thing. Would these people ever understand that he needed to run, run, run?

He did stop for a second when Lizzie said "no". He gazed up at her with his head cocked to one side. He looked like he was asking "Who, me?" His black eyes were shiny. His right ear stood straight up, and his left ear flopped over. His whiskers were twitching. Rascal looked as if he could really understand what she was saying, even if he couldn't answer.

Lizzie felt her heart melt. This sweet, smart, wild puppy really deserved to find a wonderful, loving home. But if he couldn't learn to behave, who would ever take him?

"OK, good job, everybody," Jamie was saying.

Lizzie and Jack exchanged a look. They knew she didn't mean Rascal when she said "everybody".

The other puppies weren't perfect, either. For example, Bullwinkle the bulldog absolutely hated to walk on a leash. His owner would tug on the leash, but Bullwinkle would not budge, not even an inch. The bulldog's wrinkly, flat face made him look so stubborn that Lizzie had to laugh.

Trixie the corgi had a habit of sneaking up on other puppies and stealing their toys. No matter how many of her own toys her owners brought along – fluffy ones, squeaky ones, balls, tug toys – Trixie always liked the other puppies' toys better.

But Rascal was the worst. By far. It was as if he always had to be the centre of attention. He couldn't stand it when Jamie talked for too long, or when one of the other puppies was being praised. He would bark and jump and scurry around. Lizzie had to pick him up so he would calm down.

"How is he doing at home?" Jamie asked. She had come up to Lizzie and Jack during a short break. She reached down to scratch Rascal under the chin, which made him wag his tail as hard as he could.

Lizzie sighed. "Well, he's not chewing as many things," she said. "But that's only because he's kind of locked up in the kitchen most of the time."

"He's learning to come when we call his name," Jack reported. "Remember, Lizzie? He did it yesterday, five times in a row."

"That's true," Lizzie agreed. "He really is very smart. He just has so much energy!"

Jamie nodded thoughtfully. "He may just need lots and lots of exercise and room to run," she said. She looked around the gym and saw that the other owners were back from break. "All right," she said, walking back to the middle of the circle. "Let's ask our dogs to stay."

Lizzie groaned. Not loudly enough for Jamie to hear, just a little tiny groan. So far, Rascal was not doing too well with the "stay" thing.

"Remember, we want to help the dogs do well. So we're going to start by asking them to stay only for about two seconds," Jamie said. "If they manage that, we'll give them a treat and lots of praise. Then next time, we'll ask for three seconds!"

She had the owners face their puppies, holding the leash. A few of the puppies looked up at the owners, waiting to see what they wanted. But Rascal – like most of the puppies – looked off in another direction, distracted by every noise and smell.

This place was great! Rascal loved being around all the other dogs. But what was the point if he couldn't play with them? What could possibly be more important than playing?

"OK, now ask your dog to sit," said Jamie.

"Sit!" chorused all the owners. Four dogs sat. But the Lab puppy fell down and rolled over. Rascal started barking and jumping up and down. The Alsation puppy backed up and stood there, twitching his big ears and staring at Rascal. The dachshund sniffed the floor. Jack, whose turn it was to hold Rascal's leash, looked helplessly at Lizzie.

Jamie ignored Rascal. "Great!" she said. "Now, put your hand out and raise the palm so it's facing the dog. Now tell your dog to stay."

"Stay!" everyone said. Jack said it, too. Lizzie doubted whether Rascal could hear the command. The puppy was too busy barking.

"And one, and two, and – *OK*!" said Jamie.

All the dog owners said the release word – "OK!" – and the dogs jumped up, tails wagging.

Rascal just kept bouncing and barking.

"Well, I think that's about all the time we have tonight," Jamie said, checking the clock on the wall. "See you all next time!"

Lizzie and Jack were heading outside when Jamie stopped them at the door. "I really hate to say this," she said, with a very serious look on her face, "but I don't think Rascal is . . . well, I don't think he's fitting in here. I thought we could help him, but he is making it hard for the other dogs to learn. I'm afraid I have to ask you not to bring him to class any more."

Lizzie looked down at her sneakers. She'd known this was going to happen. Rascal was getting kicked out of puppy kindergarten.

"If you'd like, you can bring him in for some private lessons," Jamie went on, in a gentle voice. "But to tell you the truth, he'd need a ton of training to be the right dog for a normal house and family. He may need a different kind of home."

Lizzie looked at her, and then down at Rascal.

What was Jamie saying? Did she mean that Rascal could *never* learn to behave? But then how could the Petersons ever find him a good home? What kind of foster family *were* they, if they couldn't help Rascal?

Rascal wondered why the people were being so serious. They had been having such a good time! Jumping and barking and playing. Why was the girl looking at him that way?

Chapter Seven

"This is so awesome!" Maria said. She and Lizzie were standing in the stable, putting Sally's saddle on again. "I can't believe your parents let you sign up for riding lessons."

"They said I deserved it because I've been working so hard with Rascal," Lizzie said. She patted Sally's neck and the old mare nickered softly. Lizzie was happy to be back at the stable.

"Is he learning to behave?" Maria asked as she tugged on a stirrup.

"Not really," Lizzie admitted. "Mum gave me and Jack one more week to try to teach him indoor manners. After that, she said we'll have to give him to the Humane Society and hope they can find him a home."

Maria shook her head. "That wouldn't be good," she said. "You can give him a lot more attention. But you'll figure something out. I'm sure of it! You're so great with dogs."

"I *was* great with dogs," Lizzie said. "But this one . . . I don't know."

"Well, forget about Rascal for a little while," Maria said. "Let's think about horses instead."

"Sounds good," said Lizzie.

"Sally's just about ready for you to ride," Maria said. "Why don't you go grab my extra helmet from the tack room while I tack up Major?" Major was Maria's favourite horse, a shiny chestnut with a white star on his forehead.

After she got the helmet, Lizzie wandered down the stable aisle, waiting for Maria. She said hello to some of the horses she'd met the other day: Treasure, Jasper, Willie. She even patted Minx, the beautiful palomino. But she stayed away from Jet, the black horse that Maria had called "skittish". Lizzie wasn't sure what that meant, but it might have something to do with kicking or biting. Lizzie was getting used to horses. She wasn't nearly as scared of them as she had been, but she still thought it was best to be careful.

Then Lizzie looked down to the last stall and caught a glimpse of a glossy brown horse. It had a big, noble head and soft, dark eyes that met Lizzie's with curiosity. "Wow," Lizzie said. She didn't know much about horses, but she could tell at a glance that this one was special. She started walking towards its stall. The horse tossed its head and whinnied as she approached. She stopped for a mument. But then she couldn't resist moving closer.

There was a sudden booming noise. Lizzie stopped in her tracks. What was *that*?

"Lizzie, stop!" Maria called from the other end of the aisle. "Don't go any closer!"

Lizzie backed up a few steps, keeping her eye on the horse, who was now tossing its head again. The whites of its eyes were showing and its ears were pointed back. Lizzie knew that when a dog's ears looked like that it was often scared or mad. That was probably true for horses, too.

Maria ran up to Lizzie. "That's Sir Galahad," she said. "Isn't he gorgeous?"

Lizzie nodded. He was the most beautiful horse she had ever seen. His glossy brown coat was gleaming, and his black mane and tail were long and silky. "Is he – dangerous?" she asked.

Maria shook her head. "No, he's just cranky. That noise you heard? He was kicking the sides of his stall."

Lizzie was glad he wasn't kicking *her*. Sir Galahad was a big horse. He seemed twice as big as Sally. "Why's he kicking?"

"He's just been a big old grouch lately," Maria said. "He's Kathy's horse. He's an amazing jumper. She used to show him all the time, but now he's so moody that she doesn't take him to horse shows. I think he's bored, and that just makes him grouchier."

"You're probably right," someone said. It was Kathy, joining them near Sir Galahad's stall. She walked right up to the big horse and rubbed his nose. He snorted but didn't move away. "Silly guy," she said. "Why can't you be nice like you used to be?"

Lizzie sighed. "It's so hard to get animals to do what you want them to do," she said.

Kathy gave her a curious look. "That's definitely true," she said. "But what animal are you having trouble with? Not Sally! She's a star."

"No," Lizzie said. "It's this puppy my family is fostering." She told Kathy a little bit about Rascal. Kathy listened and nodded.

"My husband, Wayne, and I used to have a Jack Russell," she said. "Pepper. He was kind of the stable mascot. Did you know that you can often find Jack Russells at stables? They seem to get along well with horses. Anyway, Pepper died six months ago. I still miss him like crazy, the little devil." She laughed. "Those dogs are *so* energetic.

It makes them hard to train, even though they're so smart."

That made Lizzie feel better.

Kathy thought for a moment. "Would you like to bring your little guy here next time? Maybe if I met him I could help with some training ideas."

"Really?" Lizzie asked. She had already started to have another of her great ideas. Maybe Kathy would want to adopt Rascal! He could live at the stable, with plenty of room to run and play – and get lots of attention, too. Lizzie could not imagine a better home for the little pup. "That would be awesome. Are you sure?"

Kathy nodded. "I know it will make me sad to see a Jack Russell. Wayne and I have already decided if we ever get another dog it will be a different breed. We could never replace Pepper. But still, it sounds like you could use some help with this little Rascal."

"I definitely can," Lizzie said. Her great idea had not lasted very long. It sounded like Rascal would not find a home at the stable, but it would still be fun to take him there just the same. "Thanks!"

"And now," Kathy said, "I think someone is waiting for you." She pointed down the aisle to where Sally stood patiently. "Ready for your lesson?"

Chapter Eight

When Lizzie got home from the stable she found Jack and her mum in the kitchen. She was starving. Riding definitely gave her an appetite. "What's for supper?" she asked.

She bent down to pat Rascal, who was boinging and barking. He was always so happy to see her! That felt good. When she straightened up, she saw the frown on her mother's face. And Jack had his finger over his lips, giving her the *Shh!* sign.

The Bean copied Jack, shushing Lizzie noisily. Uh-oh.

"Well," said Mum, "we *were* going to have meat loaf." She folded her arms and glared down at Rascal. "But when I was upstairs looking up recipes on the computer, *somebody* found out that he could jump high enough to reach the hamburger on the counter."

Rascal stopped bouncing for a second and sat down, looking up at them.

Why did everybody look angry? Weren't they proud of his new trick? How many dogs could jump that high? He was a very, very very good jumper, even if he did say so himself. And now that he had discovered the countertop, life in the kitchen wasn't going to be nearly as boring.

Lizzie shook her head at Rascal. He stared up at her with his black button eyes gleaming and his stubby tail wagging. How could such a naughty dog be so cute? "What are we going to do with you?" she asked.

"We're going to find him a home, that's what," Mum said.

"But Mum," Jack said. "Who will take him if he acts this way?"

Now it was Lizzie's turn to give her brother the *Shh!* sign. He was just upset because meat loaf was one of his favourite dinners. "We'll keep working on his training," she promised her mum.

"Great," said Mum. "But you need help. So I've signed us up for a private lesson with Jamie. She's coming over tonight."

"Here?" Lizzie was surprised. She didn't know that dog trainers made house calls.

"She says it's important for the whole family to learn how to train Rascal," Mum said. "She wants us all here." Mum didn't look too excited about the lesson.

Dad liked the idea, though. "It'll be fun," he said when he got home with two pizzas he'd picked up for dinner. Mum had obviously called to tell him about Rascal and the hamburger meat.

They had barely finished eating when the doorbell rang. Rascal started boinging and barking his loud, high-pitched bark. The Bean put down his pizza crust and barked along.

Mum put her hands over her ears.

Lizzie ran for the door. "Hi, Jamie," she said when she opened it.

"Hi, Lizzie," Jamie answered. "Tell you what. Let's try this again. I'll go out and wait a minute, then ring the doorbell. If Rascal starts barking—"

"He will!" Lizzie said.

"*When* Rascal starts barking," Jamie said with a smile, "try throwing this down near his feet. Don't hit him with it, and make sure he can't really tell where it's coming from." She handed Lizzie a soda can with pennies inside it and the top taped shut.

"I've used one of these before," Lizzie said, "when we were testing Shadow, the dog who is learning to be a guide dog. We tossed a penny can near Shadow to see if it would scare him. It didn't."

"Great," Jamie said. "Well, this time, the penny can is just supposed to give Rascal something else to think about. If he stops barking because he's surprised or curious, you can praise him and give him a treat."

"Let's try it!" said Lizzie. She shut the door on Jamie and went back to the kitchen. Climbing over the baby gate, she quickly explained the plan to the rest of her family. Then she stood near Rascal until the doorbell rang again.

When it did, Rascal started barking.

Lizzie threw the can.

Hey! What was that? Rascal heard the jangly noise and wondered where it came from. But he was too busy barking to stop and find out now. After all, he had a job to do. He had to let his people know that someone was at the door!

"Well, that didn't work so well," Jamie admitted when Lizzie answered the door again. "But don't worry. We'll try some other things."

Rascal was still barking as Lizzie and Jamie came into the kitchen.

"Rascal!" Dad yelled. "Cut it out!"

Dad was not usually a yeller. But everybody was tired of Rascal's barking.

"I know it's frustrating," Jamie said. "But you have to try not to yell at him. Try to think like a dog. If he hears you yelling, he thinks you're just barking, too – and he'll want to bark along."

"But what else can we do?" Mum asked, taking her hands off her ears to hear Jamie's answer.

"Ignore him," Jamie suggested. "Wait until he winds down. Then praise him."

They ignored Rascal.

They ignored him some more.

He just kept barking and boinging.

"Or," Jamie said finally, "you can try spraying him with a little water, or water mixed with vinegar." She pulled a spray bottle out of her bag and sprayed Rascal when he wasn't looking.

Hey! What was that? It didn't usually rain indoors. Rascal twirled around in a circle, trying to figure out where the water was coming from.

The barking stopped.

"Ahh," said Mum.

"Finally," said Dad.

"Good dog!" Jamie said to Rascal, giving him a biscuit. "Now," she said, "maybe we can get some training done."

Jamie stayed for over an hour, working with Rascal and with the Petersons.

Rascal tried to pay attention. He really did. But it was boring to sit, and even more boring to stay. Twirling and jumping were so much more fun!

"Thanks for coming," Mum said when the exhausted Petersons said good night to Jamie.

Jamie sighed. "You're welcome. I wish I could

help more. But the truth is, Rascal may never be a great house pet."

Jack and Lizzie looked at each other.

"I'll make some phone calls," Jamie went on. "I know a lady who takes dogs on her farm. Maybe Rascal could stay with her for a while. The dogs don't get a lot of attention, but at least he would have a place to live."

Mum and Dad nodded. But Jack and Lizzie shook their heads. The farm part sounded good, but Rascal loved people and needed attention. They would have to keep trying to find him the right home – and they didn't have much time left.

Chapter Nine

"Are you sure this is a good idea?" Dad asked when he dropped Lizzie, Jack, and Rascal off at the stable the next day after school. Rascal was going to meet Kathy, and then Jack was going to watch him while Lizzie took a riding lesson.

"Kathy said I should bring him," Lizzie said. "Maybe she'll have some good ideas about training Rascal."

"OK," Dad said. "Just make sure to keep him on the leash. We don't want him getting in trouble."

Maria was waiting. "Hi, Rascal," she said, bending down to give the puppy a hug. "You are such a cutie. Kathy's going to love you."

"Where is Kathy?" Lizzie asked.

"Probably in the barn," Maria said. She led the

way into the stables. Rascal followed, pulling on the leash Lizzie was holding.

What a great place! Rascal loved all the wonderful smells. There was so much to explore here. And look! What were these huge animals? Were they giant dogs?

"Rascal likes the horses," Lizzie said, laughing as Rascal pulled her along, stopping at each stall to sniff and greet any horses who looked down to see his little face peering from under their stall doors.

Jack agreed. "He's so excited that he's not even barking!"

Rascal darted from stall to stall, tugging Lizzie behind him. Suddenly, there was a loud booming noise from the end of the aisle. "Sir Galahad!" Lizzie said. The big horse was kicking his stall walls again. She wondered if the noise would scare Rascal, but he didn't look frightened at all. In fact, he pulled even harder in that direction.

"He wants to meet Sir Galahad," Lizzie told Jack. "But that's probably not a good idea." She could picture the little dog getting trampled by the gigantic horse – or even kicked!

Just then, Kathy stepped out of Minx's stall, carrying a pitchfork and wiping her forehead. "Whew!" she said. "Last stall of the day. Now they're all clean. Hey, is this Rascal?"

She knelt down and opened her arms, and Rascal pulled so hard that Lizzie had to let go of the leash. The little dog flew toward Kathy, licking her face as she gathered him into a hug. "Well, hello there, cutie!" she said, laughing. "Aren't you something?"

Rascal liked this lady. He liked her very, very much. She smelled so nice! And he could tell that she liked him, too.

Kathy hugged Rascal close, and Lizzie could see tears in her eyes. She knew that Kathy must be thinking of her old dog, Pepper. But Kathy was smiling, too.

"He's just darling," Kathy said finally, standing up and brushing straw off her jeans. "He's going to be bigger than my old dog and he has more brown spots than Pepper did, but I can tell he has the same personality. Always in a good mood, always curious, always looking for trouble."

"That's Rascal!" Lizzie and Jack said together. Lizzie introduced her brother.

"Welcome to the stable!" Kathy said, smiling at Jack. "You've got your hands full with this guy. Jacks aren't easy to train. But they're worth the work! Pepper was the best dog, once he decided to listen to me – at least once in a while." She sighed. Then she gave herself a little shake. "Well! Ready for your lesson?" she asked Lizzie.

"Definitely," Lizzie said.

"I think Wayne has Sally tacked up for you already," Kathy said. "Wayne?" she called down the aisle.

A man emerged from the tack room. "Sally's all set," he called back.

"Want to meet Rascal?" Kathy asked her husband.

Lizzie saw Wayne shake his head. "Busy," he said, turning around quickly and walking out of the barn.

Kathy shrugged. "Don't mind him. He just misses Pepper. They were great friends," she said. "Now, what's Rascal going to do while you and Maria ride?" she asked.

"Jack is going to watch him," Lizzie said.

Kathy gave Jack the thumbs-up. "Excellent. Let's go!" She led the way to the riding ring, where Sally was waiting.

Once Lizzie was sitting in the saddle, Kathy dropped the bombshell. "No more lead line," she said. "You're on your own today. You're the boss. You tell Sally which way to go, and how fast."

Lizzie felt her heart pound. "How fast?" she

asked. "You mean, like, I should make her trot or something?" She knew that trotting was next fastest after walking. Then came cantering and galloping. There was no way she was ready for either of those! Even trotting sounded scary, especially since she knew she would have to start learning how to post. Posting meant bouncing up and down in time with the horse's movements. Lizzie had seen Maria do it, but she had no idea how to do it herself.

"We'll start with a walk," Kathy said. "Sally's in no hurry. She could walk all day." She grinned at Lizzie. "Go on, now. Tell her to 'giddy up', and start around the ring clockwise."

Lizzie clucked her tongue and gave Sally a little kick. Then, when Sally started moving, she pulled on the outside rein the way Kathy had taught her – and Sally turned! "Wow!" Lizzie said out loud. She couldn't stop smiling. She was riding!

Lizzie forgot everything for the next half-hour.

She was concentrating so hard on her lesson that she probably wouldn't have noticed if the barn stood up and walked away.

But she did notice when Jack started shouting. "Rascal!" he yelled. "Rascal, where are you?"

The little spotted dog was nowhere in sight.

Chapter Ten

"Jack!" Lizzie said, pulling Sally over to the fence that ran around the riding ring. "Where's Rascal?" From up on the horse, she looked down at her brother. He looked very small – and his face was very white.

"I – I don't know," Jack admitted. "I got tired of holding him, and he was being pretty good. You were busy riding, but Kathy said I could tie him to the fence." He pointed to a fence post near the gate. "I went to watch Maria riding over in the other ring and – now he's gone!"

Lizzie could tell that Jack felt awful. "It's not your fault," she told him.

By then, Kathy was at Jack's side. "Don't worry,"

she said, putting an arm around his shoulders. "We'll find Rascal." She looked up at Lizzie. "I think our lesson's over for today," she said. "Want help getting down?"

Lizzie shook her head. "That's OK," she said. She knew how to dismount by now. She pulled her right foot out of the stirrup and slid off Sally's back.

"I'll bring Sally back into the barn," Lizzie said. "Maybe Rascal's in there. I think he liked all the horses."

"Good," Kathy said. "You look there. Jack and I will start checking some other places."

As she led Sally away, Lizzie found herself wishing she would hear Rascal's bark. It seemed as if the stable was the only place he was quiet. She hadn't heard him bark once since he arrived. If only he were barking now, they could find him!

It took a mument for her eyes to adjust to the darkness of the stable. She led Sally to her stall. "Wait here," she told the mare. "We'll come back and get your saddle off in a minute, as soon as we find that bad little puppy!"

She gave Sally's neck a pat and closed her stall door carefully. Then she headed down the aisle, checking each stall to see if Rascal had wriggled underneath the door for a visit. He wasn't with Willie, or Jasper, or Treasure. Minx was alone in her stall and so was Jet.

Lizzie listened for the booming sound of Sir Galahad's kicks, but the barn was quiet.

"What's going on?" Maria asked, hurrying up the aisle. She was still wearing her helmet. "I just heard that Rascal is missing!"

Lizzie nodded. "I'm checking the stalls," she said. She started walking fast towards the end of the aisle. Rascal had been interested in Sir Galahad before. What if he had gone into the big horse's stall? Why was the grouchy horse's stall so quiet?

Maria saw where she was going. "Oh, no!" she said. "Do you think –"

"I sure hope not," Lizzie said.

Both girls hurried down to the last stall. "Empty!" Lizzie said when she looked inside. Rascal wasn't there – and neither was Sir Galahad!

"Galahad's out in the paddock," Wayne said, coming up behind them. "I thought he needed some exercise and fresh grass, since he was so bored."

"I wonder if that's where Rascal is, too!" Lizzie said.

"The dog is missing?" Wayne asked. He followed Lizzie and Maria as they ran outside and around the back of the barn to the paddock.

They arrived at the fence at the same time as Jack and Kathy.

"There's Sir Galahad," said Maria, pointing. The big horse stood grazing calmly in the shade of a tall tree.

"And there's Rascal!" said Lizzie. She couldn't believe her eyes. The puppy was lying in the shade right next to one of Sir Galahad's big hooves. He looked completely contented and relaxed. Lizzie had never seen him that way before!

"He's all tuckered out," Kathy said.

"But he might get kicked!" Jack said.

"I doubt it," Wayne said slowly. "Sir Galahad looks pretty happy to have him there."

Lizzie thought she'd better call him, anyway. "Rascal!" she shouted. The one thing she had taught the puppy to do was to come when he was called. Sure enough, he jumped to his feet and began to trot over to the crowd at the fence, trailing his leash behind him.

Sir Galahad looked up at the puppy. He took one more bite of grass and then trotted after Rascal. Lizzie saw Kathy and Wayne look at each other in surprise.

The horse and the dog arrived together at the fence. Rascal jumped up to put both front feet on the railing near Lizzie. He poked his nose through and gave her a lick on the cheek when she bent down to pick up his leash.

Hi! Hi! Hi! Rascal was so happy to see his old friend. He wondered how she liked his new friend! This place was the best place Rascal had ever been. He loved it here! He licked the girl again, to thank her for bringing him here.

Meanwhile, Sir Galahad was gently nosing at the pocket of Kathy's coat. "Is this what you want?" she asked, pulling out a carrot. She gave it to him and he took it gently. His ears were standing up straight as he nickered and nodded in thanks.

"Wow," Kathy said to Wayne. "I haven't seen him so happy since—"

"Since Pepper was around," Wayne said, finishing his wife's sentence. "Why didn't we realize it before? He just missed his friend, that's all. That's why he was so cranky!"

Wayne reached down to scratch Rascal on the head. "You're a good little guy," he said softly.

Lizzie looked at Jack with her eyebrows raised. He nodded. So did Maria, who understood what Lizzie was thinking.

"Go for it," urged Maria in a whisper.

Lizzie took a deep breath. "You know," she said to Kathy and Wayne, "Rascal seems really happy here at the stable. He may never have great inside manners, but he behaves well when he has plenty of room and lots of interesting things to do and see."

Kathy was nodding. Lizzie saw her reach out to take Wayne's hand. Wayne looked over at Kathy before gazing down at the puppy again.

"So – " Lizzie went on, "would you like to adopt him?"

She didn't even have to wait for the answer. She saw the smiles on their faces as they both knelt down to pat Rascal.

The troublesome little puppy had found a home – the best home in the world for him.

Lizzie felt a little twinge of sadness. Rascal may have been a handful, but she had become attached to his cute face and wild ways. Would she always have to say goodbye to the puppies they fostered? Or would one of them finally come to stay? Lizzie hoped that someday she and Jack and the Bean would have a dog of their very own. But for now she just had to be happy that they had found the very best place for Rascal.

PUPPY TipS

All dogs are wonderful, but not every dog is right for every family. Before you fall in love with a certain breed, it's a good idea to learn more about its personality and needs.

A big, athletic dog is not the best choice for people who live in small city apartments. Some breeds are better for families with young children, and some get along with cats, while others don't. Some dogs like to swim and others would rather run. And for people who like a very clean home, there are even some dogs who don't moult!

You can find out more about different breeds from books or on the Internet. Do the research with an adult. Then discuss what you learn with the whole family before deciding which kind of dog is best for you.

Dear Reader,

I think Jack Russell terriers are adorable, but like Lizzie, I prefer big dogs. My dog, Django (the D is silent so you say it "Jango"), is an especially big black Labrador retriever. He's very tall, with long legs and a long body.

When people see him, they always say, "Boy, that dog is big!"

Sometimes I miss the days when he was a puppy and he could fit in my lap. If Django tried to get in my lap now, he would squash me!

My friend Annie has two miniature poodles, and both of them can fit in my lap at once. I guess there are some good things about small dogs.

Do you like big dogs or little dogs better? Why?

Yours from the Puppy Place,
Ellen Miles

For Jamie

First published in the US by Scholastic Inc., 2006
This edition published in the UK by Scholastic Ltd, 2007
Scholastic Children's Books
An imprint of Scholastic Ltd
Euston House, 24 Eversholt Street
London, NW1 1DB, UK
Registered office: Westfield Road, Southam, Warwickshire, CV47 0RA
SCHOLASTIC and associated logos are trademarks and or registered trademarks of
Scholastic Inc.

10 digit ISBN 0 439 95530 0
13 digit ISBN 978 0439 95530 0

British Library Cataloguing-in-Publication Data.
A CIP catalogue record for this book is available from the British Library

Printed and bound by CPI Group (UK) Ltd, Croydon, CR0 4YY
Papers used by Scholastic Children's Books are made from wood grown in
sustainable forests.

18 20 19

www.scholastic.co.uk/zone

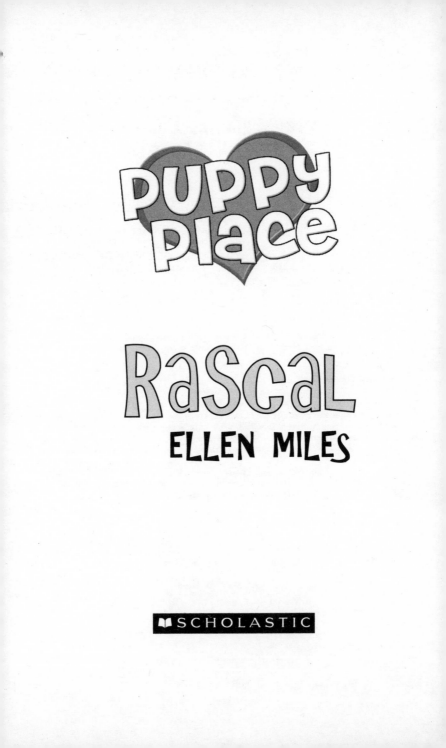

PUPPY PLACE

RASCAL

ELLEN MILES

SCHOLASTIC